The Second 100

A COLLECTION OF ONE HUNDRED WORD STORIES

ERICA L. DRAYTON

ISBN: 978-1-7339259-2-1

Book Cover by Erica L. Drayton.

First edition 2024.

The Second 100

ERICA L. DRAYTON

dedication

For Dax.

introduction

The First 100 seems so long ago, especially when I think back to the early days of coming up with stories on the fly. I realized pretty early on that the key to not only writing a great story, but being able to deliver on daily was themes.

Within the next 100 stories I borrow inspiration from fellow newsletter writers of fiction, literary classics, and a desire to reconnect with pen and paper as well.

By the time I finished writing these stories the sky was the limit and what was once a daily task has quickly become a habit.

"Short stories are tiny windows into other worlds and other minds and other dreams. They are journeys you can make to the far side of the universe and still be back in time for dinner."

— Neil Gaiman

The Second 100

Nowhere Island

#101

"Everyone have a phone ready?" Nine people in the room pull out their phones and hold them up in the air. A large 80' screen comes to life at the far end of the room.

Projected on the screen is the face of a complete stranger to everyone in the room. He is breathing heavily, sweating, and looks absolutely terrified. The sun is about to set on Nowhere Island.

"Ladies and gentlemen, meet Frank. Thirty-two years old. Widowed. Stock broker. No children." Some groan with disappointment, while others are excited. "Will he survive the first night? Place your bets now."

Branded

#102

We've been on the run for five days and nights. I sleep. My mother doesn't. There is fear in her eyes. My thirteenth birthday passed five days ago but unlike my brother I didn't get a cake. Instead, I was woken up in the middle of the night and taken away.

She believes there's a place I can go to be free. If we stay I will be branded just like my mother.

She puts her hair up in a bun to cool off. I can see a letter burned into the back of her neck, glistening by the moonlight.

The Park

#103

An elderly woman walks to the park. The same route for the past eighty-two years of her life. Memories of walking with her mother. Holding hands as they crossed the road.

A lover whispers in her ear naughty words that make her blush as they lean against an old oak tree.

She tries to hold her daughter's hand. An act her daughter hated. She pulls away and runs into a busy road. A tear rolls down her cheek.

The park is empty save for that old oak tree. She can't sit beneath it anymore. But she visits for the memories.

Pirates

#104

The pirates were gaining on me. I wasn't surprised. A raft made out of trees and fastened with bamboo wasn't going to outrun anything in the open seas. But I had my best friend, Skamp, and the wind on my side.

Suddenly, I heard cannon fire behind me. The enemy fast approaching. I thought they missed till the ripple effect capsized my raft and I flailed, taking in water, struggling to find the surface for air.

Skamp licked my face, waking me from an adventurous dream. On the floor of my bedroom, tangled in bedsheets, not a pirate in sight.

Twins

#105

The band began to play a slow song while hundreds of party guests stood around, waiting for the moment. They were all invited to the Miller home to witness their eldest daughter become engaged.

Twin brother and sister, Hannah and Gregory, spent the evening drinking and laughing together. He knew what everyone was expecting to see happen.

Hannah spotted the eldest daughter sitting alone. Waiting.

"It's now or never," Gregory said, and downed his sister's glass of champagne for her.

Hannah walked across the dance floor and extended her hand for a dance. A woman screamed and Mrs. Miller fainted.

Them

#106

They came in stages. First there was just one ship. Seemed harmless at first. We sent in our best and brightest to communicate with them. They claimed to be just passing through. Then more of them showed up.

A decade later and we're still unsure what they want from us. Government officials suggest we remain calm, but since their arrival no one has died. Normally we would be thrilled at the prospect of immortality, until overpopulation turned rational men into territorial tyrants.

There just isn't enough space for us all. Tomorrow we start boarding their ships for a new planet.

Sampson

#107

"Damn it, Sampson, how did it get out? You told me it was under lock and key. You said this place was harder to get into than Area 51. And yet, here we stand, in an empty room. How do you account for that?"

Sampson was just as surprised as his superior. There was no sign of a break in and the computer logs showed no one had opened the door since it had been placed inside.

"I…I don't know, ma'am," Sampson stammered. "Should we alert the President?"

She stared daggers into his soul and said, "no shit, Sherlock."

Usual Suspects
#108

I wanted to say "round up the usual suspects" like in the movie, but standing in the middle of a gravesite where half a dozen elderly women were buried, I knew this wasn't the time.

I puffed on my cigar and listened to my assistant, covered in mud from head to toe, recited what little information we had so far. I didn't need much to know exactly whose handy work this was. The dormant Grandma Killer had returned.

Part of me was excited. Not for the dead. But for the living, and the cold case just beginning to catch heat.

The Circus

#109

"If that's the best this hick town has to offer we're in trouble," Geronimo, the ringmaster said twirling his long black mustache. Disappointment on his face as the third act walked off stage.

"I am from here. Trust me. This town hasn't changed much. Filled with weirdos."

The circus was passing through on their way to a neighboring city. But business was no longer booming. A new act to bring the gawkers round again was desperately needed.

Just when it seemed like all hope was gone, the ground beneath them rattled. Their water filled glasses toppled over as she entered.

Zeros and Ones

#110

Frannie leaned back in her chair and smiled as she watched the series of zeros and ones scroll across her computer screen. She had spent the last 48 hours working without sleep to crack the code.

She picked up her cellphone and hit the dial button. It was answered before the first ring.

"Well?" She said, waiting for an answer.

"Your reputation precedes you, kid."

"Yeah. Yeah. I know. Cut the bullshit. My money?"

"Sent." They hung up without another word. She opened her bank app and saw a new deposit of five million dollars. Then her computer screen froze.

The Voice

#111

Her implant began to malfunction over a month ago. Instead of the usual voice she heard in her ear since birth, there was nothing. She didn't understand this aloneness. But she didn't want to report it either. Every day she spent with her own thoughts made her feel more alive.

At work she pretended to hear the voice. It told her to take more breaks. Watch more movies. Listen to more music. Her co-workers and neighbors began to get suspicious as their voice never told them to do those things.

She made plans to run away to the voiceless land.

Any Bear

#112

One day while plowing his fields, a farmer hears an animal in distress. He finds a bear trapped beneath a fallen tree. Without hesitation he manages to move the tree and the bear survives.

The following week, the farmer notices dark clouds rolling in. Signs that a storm is approaching. He rushes to his barn to secure his animals, then home. He decides wading across a knee-high creek would be faster, but he loses his footing and falls, hitting his head on a rock.

A bear nearby sees it happen and runs off to find shelter, as any bear would.

Infomercian

#113

Five reasons why you should never bury a body in the middle of a rain storm:

1. The body will be twice as heavy.
2. Serial killers never ask for help to carry the body.
3. Shoveling mud exerts too much energy.
4. If the victim has friends or relatives, they are more likely to check-in on their well-being during times of inclement weather or natural disasters.
5. No matter how deep you dig, the rain will always uncover the truth.

Act now to get our pocket-sized "checklist for murder" and get it right every time or your money back.

Dead End

#114

A flat tire made me do it. Knock on the door of a cottage nestled at the end of a dead end street. The proprietor was pleasant enough. He let me use the phone in his study. There were books on the shelves about anatomy with a mix of horror and mystery classics.

The tow company couldn't get to me till the next morning. In hindsight, I probably should've slept in my car.

The hairs on the back of my neck told me I was being watched. I wasn't sure until I crept down to the basement where I found—

Sentence

#115

My sentence was the most severe of them all. I tried a plea deal for a lethal injection but was denied. Instead I would serve out my life in Chokeville. The worst place on Earth for any self-respecting serial killer.

There are those who may think we're getting off easy, being forced to live together on an island. But what fun is killing if your next door neighbor sees you coming a mile away?

Tomorrow I'm to be transferred to the shipyard where a ferry will take me to my final resting place. If I'm lucky the ship will sink.

The Bells

#116

"…she called the tower her home—"

"But couldn't she just take the stairs?" Tim asked, a look of concern on his face.

"Let's keep reading and maybe your question will be answered," his mother said, as she read, "She wanted to take the stairs but her door was locked. The only way out was through her window."

"What did she do, mommy?" The bell tower rang out the first of twelve bells. She looked at her son and smiled.

"We'll find out tomorrow," she said, kissed him on the forehead and closed the door on the empty room behind her.

Clouds

#117

"And you're sure it's her time? I didn't get the memo," Zeke said, looking down from their perch in the clouds at Esther Jones in her garden, taking a nap on a lawn chair, hat shielding her face from the midday sun.

"Yes, well, when you've been in the business long enough, you go on instinct," Raker said. "You'll learn. Now go on so we can grab lunch after. I'm starving."

Zeke tumbled out of the clouds, his wings spread instantly as he landed beside Esther. He extended his hand and she grabbed him by the wrist.

"Not today, angel."

The Hog

#118

"This is the story of a lifetime, Jerry. It's the kind that takes a nothing paper like The 'Hog' and turns it into a real household name instead of highly recommended by fishermen's wives."

Jerry teetered in her chair, feet propped up on the desk, considering her options in silence. She shook her head and pulled a cigarette from the inside pocket of her suit jacket.

"No dice, Trev. I'm through with this life. The 'Hog' is gonna have to sizzle without me. I'm moving on to bigger and better."

"Nothing is better than the 'Hog,' and you know it."

The Game

#119

No one had ever beaten this game in less than thirteen moves. It was impossible. Even the most advanced computers in the world couldn't come up with a win in less than thirteen moves.

All of that changed one night on international television. The entire world was watching. Each opponent moved methodically with each turn. Beads of sweat could be seen on both, bright lights overhead, every camera angle ready to capture it all.

An audible gasp came from the spectators and in homes all over the world after the eleventh move. Everyone knew history was about to be made.

The Necklace

#120

"Gather round, children," Elder Sarah said from her family room, a pipe dangling from her mouth. She wore a black and red checkered house dress and a necklace made of bones that rattled as she leaned back in her rocking chair.

Three young children sat at her feet and listened as she spun a tale their parent's were told when they were children. When she had finished, the youngest pointed to her necklace and asked, "Why do you wear a necklace made of bones around your neck?"

"These are the fingers of children, not unlike you three, who were disobedient."

NO EXIT

#121

"If you'll just sign here. Here," she paused as I hastily signed my name on every line she pointed out. "And here." She smiled at me and my mouth suddenly yearned for a glass of water. My god. What have I done?

She pushed a blue button I hadn't noticed before and two large men in ill-fitting lab coats appeared through a door labeled "NO EXIT."

"If you just follow these gentlemen, they will take good care of you." Her voice was calm and so reassuring. I no longer wondered if I made the right decision, signing away my brain.

Sober

#122

She exited the Rusty Anchor about as gracefully as one would expect anyone who'd spent the entire evening accepting free drinks from stranger men. Her stiletto heels made it impossible for her to take a steady step so she removed them.

Feeling the cold cobblestones beneath her stocking feet brought sobriety just in time to feel the hairs on the back of her neck get all prickly. This was not an uncommon occurrence. She gripped one heel in each hand. Bracing for anything.

The tenements were just a few blocks away. She heard footfalls quicken as she started to run.

The End

#123

She ripped the page from her notebook, then crumpled and threw it at her wastepaper basket, surrounded by dozens of similar failed attempts. Her notebook had just a few sheets remaining.

"This is so stupid," she muttered to herself.

She wrote the word THE and stared at it till it lost all meaning. Her doctors said writing was the best medicine, in their professional opinion.

"Don't let an accident stop you," they said. Her award winning books taunting her on the shelves. She wanted to scream. The words just wouldn't come anymore.

Then she wrote END, and that was enough.

The Carriage

#124

The horses hooves on the cobblestones echoed down the dark and empty street pulling an empty carriage. The driver steadied their pace to a trot, admiring the full moon and stars. In the distance, standing under a dimly lit street lamp, was a woman of questionable character, smoking a cigarette.

Behind her, lurking in the shadows, stood a man watching. Waiting. The horses sped up. From a trot to a gallop the driver veered to the left, the carriage struck the woman in an instant.

The man stepped out of the shadows and blew his whistle.

"After her!" he shouted.

Jars

#125

His eyes darted around the room but he couldn't move or speak.

"I can see you're worried. Don't be. You see, I've done this before," she whispered through her masked face at a naked man strapped to a gurney under a dim light.

She moved to a tall bookcase. His eyes followed as she pulled a cord and drapes parted, revealing shelves of jars. Each containing a heart.

"I loved them all. But none compare to you." He looked down at his chest and saw black lines. She hovered over him, a scalpel in hand. "This might leave a scar."

The Card Game

#126

"Are you sure about that bid, Harold?" Sally asked, grinning innocently at her partner who studied his cards again, then tapped his fingers on the table.

"Oh no you don't. No signaling to each other with some sort of code," Jim said.

"Speak for yourself. Sally and I know you two cheat. We just haven't figured out how." They all laugh out loud.

"Welcome holiday shoppers! This weekend we have a sale on card tables for you and the whole family…"

A curtain parts revealing four mannequins sitting around a card table, playing Spades, with painted smiles on their faces.

Breakfast

#127

"Are you sure now is the right time?"

"Quit shaking your leg. You'll bring attention to us," he said, calm and cold. "You've paid me half. When it's done you'll pay me the rest and I'll be on my way."

"Yes, but…what if he—" Before she could finish the man got up from the booth and walked towards the exit just as my usual plate of breakfast arrived.

The thought crossed my mind, briefly, that I ought to say something to the proper authorities? Right after I've eaten. Breakfast is the most important meal of the day, after all.

The Butcher

#128

The man is obsessed with me. Every time I come in he's staring at me. Never watching what he's doing. But he's the only butcher for miles. And a house cannot run without meat to nourish the souls that live within.

Today the shop is packed with customers. I am fourth in line, but that doesn't stop his eyes from trying to catch mine. He raises his cleaver in the air and brings it down with purpose, narrowly missing his fingers. His eyes never leaving mine. A perfectly cut rump for the gentleman.

The next chop isn't quite so lucky.

Siren Song

#129

"These shores are not to be reckoned with, mum. Best to keep the lamps burnin', if yer catch me meanin'," Smythe said, leaning in so close his breath made her eyes water.

"Nonsense. It's an old pirate tale. A mermaid scared of light?" she questioned, as clouds covered the full moon.

"MERMAIDS UP AHEAD!" shouted the crewman from the lookout. He pointed a shaky finger towards the black murky waters while the men strained to catch a glimpse of her.

All except the woman. There are no such things as mermaids, she thought, until their siren song called to her.

Beast

#130

Every night I dream I'm running through the woods at night. Dark and mysterious. I've never been there before yet it feels like it's my home. The ground beneath my bare feet is wet from rain. I'm being chased by something in the dark. I can hear its heavy breathing and low growl behind me. A beast?

I know I'm dreaming. If I can just make myself wake up then I'll be safe. My chest is tight with fear as—

—suddenly I'm falling. Above me I can see stars in the sky. The wind against my face just before I—

Rehearsals

#131

"Oh sweet scented apple. Temptress off the vine—," she stopped short. "Sid, this line doesn't work. Apples don't grow on vines. They grow on trees. Who wrote this crap, anyway?"

"I did," Sid, the writer and director, seethed through gritted teeth. No one uttered a word. Waiting. "Fine. You may say 'branch' but please bite the damn apple so we can all go on break." She nodded. "Lights!"

"Oh sweet scented apple. Temptress of the branch," she said, taking a bite. She grabbed her throat and collapsed.

"This is why we have rehearsals," he said, standing over the dead body.

Rebecca

#132

Rebecca came to live with us when she was seven. Her records burned down in a fire at her previous orphanage. But she needed a home and we had plenty of room and time to devote to a child.

One day I woke up to find her standing by the side of my bed, eyes closed, sinister smile on her face.

Her doctor mentioned night terrors but died of unknown causes soon after.

Now, whenever I'm making dinner I feel the hairs on the back of my neck stand. She's watching me. And the butcher knife's been missing for days…

Magic

#133

I clink my champagne glass to get all of my guests attention. "I'm sure you're all wondering why I asked you here? Half of you hate me, while the other half I hate."

They stared at each other. No one daring to look me in the eye.

"I could think of no one I'd want to share my glorious news with. Those who would appreciate it more, of course." I waited a moment before announcing, "I'm dying. Drink up."

I raise my glass and everyone else raises their glass to drink with me.

"And I'm taking you all with me."

Paint

#134

My hands were stained with paints from decades of pain and suffering. Each piece, a part of me. Keeping me awake till I finish what I started.

A week of no sleep can make any man start to see things in the swirls that weren't there before.

Am I dreaming on my feet? With each new color introduced a memory extracted. Put on display for all the world or no one to see.

A streak of red for blood. White for bone. I mix the lights with the darks to get the black I need. My truth in the shadows.

Generosity

#135

"I am in a generous mood. Which makes this your lucky day. Normally, when I'm hired to do a job, I do it right."

Unable to move, his captive just listened, tied to a chair by his hands and legs. A gag in his mouth.

"I've had others try to escape. Run away. It only delayed the inevitable. But not you. When I showed up you surrendered without question. As if you knew I was coming? So today, I'm going to kill you instantly rather than leave you awake while I dismember your body and pop you in the post."

Illumination

#136

She waited till the last person came out of the pool and left the building before climbing the stairs to the diving board. It had been years since she dared to swim in public and while this was a public pool she still waited till there was no one around.

Her first bounce was wobbly and she steadied herself. Her nerves got the better of her.

She raised her arms in the air, gave one good bounce and dove off the board into the water. Her eyes opened and light burst forth, turning the water into a shimmering blue green.

Past Due

#137

The room was dark and dank. Not what I was expecting at all. The elevator operator cleared his throat, waiting for me to exit.

As I took my first step a light came on over a large desk in the middle of the room. Sitting behind the desk was a woman. Her hair in a bun, red lipstick, heavy makeup, and thick glasses.

She pointed a manicured finger at a chair I hadn't noticed there before.

"Let's see here," she said as I sat down slowly. "It appears you're past due on your payments. You owe us two dead bodies."

Another Time

#138

I woke up this morning in a bed different from my own, beside a stranger. I try to remember my past but all I see are flashes of a life I barely recognize.

Unsure of my surroundings I slip out of bed, in search of a wallet for identification. Perhaps it will jog my memory. Either that or I'm in some strange nightmare.

I walk past a mirror in the hall and catch a glimpse of my face. I recognize it. My name. My other life. This isn't a different place, it's another time.

I'm older but none the wiser.

Dylan

#139

"In a world where rules don't exist and everything is planned. Chaos never reigns. It dominates."

"Finish your breakfast, young man. Or the only chaos you'll encounter is from your mother."

Dylan ate everything and scampered from the table before she could hand out chores. He knew his enemy was lurking just around the corner.

"In a world where cats are ferocious beasts, Dylan isn't afraid. He's faced down a tabby or two in his day. And he can do it—"

As Dylan expected, the neighborhood cat was waiting for him. He curled his mouse tail, ready for the chase.

Camp

#140

The embers crackled in the still night air. A family of three sat around a fire that wasn't theirs, sipping from mugs.

"I think they's ready, maw. Can we eat now?"

"Weasel, I done tole ya we gotta let the meat marinate as long as possible. Really lock in the flavor," his mother cackled.

Weasel sulked while he drank his mug of blood.

"Ham, go see if they ready. Yer brother fixin' to pass out from hunger."

Ham walked over to a tent and looked in. Three bodies crammed in a large barrel.

"They look ready to eat!" he shouted.

Wine

#141

"I found this old bottle of wine when I moved in. Says it was bottled in 1480," I said, handing over the dust covered bottle.

"1480? That's impossible," Kerri, my best friend, said, and grabbed it from me. She held it up to the light to see if there was anything inside. Once confirmed she handed it back and I proceeded to wriggle the cork till it came free with the familiar POP.

I would describe the smell it released as floral. But seeing as now we're both six feet under, that's all I feel like sharing at this time.

The Dance

#142

The music coming from Hanover House was so loud the ground at the cemetery vibrated. The house was filled with guests in costume, drinking and laughing and dancing to the music. No one noticed the couple who floated a few inches off the floor when they moved.

They wore their wedding attire from the blessed day that took place nearly a century ago in this very house. He was much smaller in his tuxedo and she didn't fill out her dress quite like she used to.

Their skeletal faces shone by the lights of the disco ball. And they danced.

Nameless

#143

The old man sat in the church cemetery every single day clutching a bunch of lilies in one hand and his hat in the other. His hair balding on top but the wisps of auburn, a nod to his younger years.

The bench he occupied faced several gravestones but it was one in particular he visited. Large rectangle. Same as the rest. But upon further inspection, what made it different from the others was its lack of a name.

Only he knew who was buried there and as long as he lived he vowed to keep watch and never forget.

The Expedition

#144

Field Guide Log #84

We had been underground for hours, walking through a web of tunnels before finding what we were looking for. A large stone with images believed to be the first story written by human hands. We scanned the images, hoping to be the first to transcribe it for the world.

They told the story of a woman who was chased by beasts. She entered a cave, not unlike ours, and hid away, waiting to be rescued.

"I knew you'd come." The voice was faint but definitely female. We came for a story but uncovered so much more.

Confessions

#145

"…it's been ten days since my last confession. I killed a man last night. And it felt good. To be honest, he had it coming from the very beginning."

Making my confession made me feel so much better. A weight had been lifted, telling a man who had to keep my secret.

"I understand, my child," he said, and paused before adding, "will you do it again?"

"I think so. I can't help it. I have a taste for it now. What should I do?"

"Go home and finish the story so I can read how it ends, of course!"

Race

#146

A hot tip. That's what it was. So hot, in fact, he began to sweat. Eating lunch one afternoon he overheard a conversation he wouldn't dare repeat to anyone.

There were five men in front of him. Unable to be still and patient he started to bite his nails. Now four men.

The race was about to begin and he still hadn't placed his bet.
Now three men.
His mouth was suddenly like the Sahara desert, palms sticky.
Two men.

He reached in his pocket.

One man.

No wallet.

Panic set in. A shot rang out to start the race.

Charlatan

#147

"Come one, come all! Have I got a remedy for you! Ailments? I've got the cure!" His voice echoed through the small, quiet, village as he held tightly the reigns on a horse pulling his carriage that rattled along the cobblestones.

"Come one, come all! Have I got—" He stopped short when he saw a woman standing in front of the local saloon, full petticoat, ringlets of auburn curls, and a rifle resting over one shoulder.

"I wouldn't stop here if I were you, mister. Our cemetery's full of your kind." She lowered her rifle and aimed it at him.

Hiatus

#148

After a decade hiatus from writing, I felt it was time to get back to my typewriter. Surely, no one would remember what happened the last time. Especially, since I've taken the necessary precautions with my writing room.

It was a dark and stormy night...

I looked through the bars of my four by six inch window in the basement at the sudden flash in the sky.

...when a body, held under water by weights came loose over time, walked out of the water.

My fingers twitched over the keys as the sound of wet footsteps bounced off the walls.

Scrupulous

#149

"I take pride in my work. It's why customers are willing to pay three times what my competitors charge just to get a meeting with me. I'm the best at what I do." She sipped her cup of coffee, seemingly unimpressed. They always play hard to get at first.

"If I wanted cheap and easy I could've gone with someone else. I'm looking for an artist. Are you...an artist?" She broke eye contact and proceeded to light a cigarette.

"My work has been featured on the cover of international newspapers. You wouldn't be sitting here talking to me otherwise."

Foible

#150

Mr. Smithers had an accident. He slipped down the stairs to his basement, shovel in one hand, flashlight in the other. When the paramedics arrived he managed to crawl to the top of the stairs. No one bothered to investigate the twelve graves down there. Or the thirteenth fresh one.

Mr. Smithers is in trouble. He's suffered a broken leg and is stuck in the hospital, recovering. There's a body in his basement, unburied, and not dead yet.

But Mr. Smithers has a wife who loves him despite his foibles. Which is why she was late getting to the hospital.

Aftermath

#151

Recent murder messier than you anticipated? Looking to get out in a hurry before the long arm of the law catches up with you? Just call Aftermath Quick Clean. We're available 365 days out of the year. All day and especially for all your late night kills.

We are the most discreet crew you'll ever find. Name never required. Cash only payments. Not a drop of blood left behind or your money back. Guaranteed.

Our packages are more than reasonable. And if you murder someone in the next hour, we'll throw in any body part as a souvenir for free!

Pungent

#152

On the morning of October 31st, head chef Sophie decided to prepare the soup. A task normally reserved for the saucier whom she fired without cause.

She worked at Au Revoir Mon Amis for over two decades. In that time she'd prepared dishes for thousands of patrons. Survived multiple management take-overs. Four terrible husbands. And today was Resignation Day.

Everyone in the kitchen noticed a pungent odor coming from the soup, but no one dare question Chef Sophie's recipe.

By the evening, twenty tables sat down to dine, starting with the soup. No one made it to the main course.

Filch

#153

Hank banged the gavel to get everyone to quiet down. "This is the 1,248th meeting of the Filch Society. James, if you can call the roll."

James cleared his throat before standing, clipboard in hand. "Trevor." All eyes turned to a man blocked by a large black trash bag on the table in front of him. He opened it to reveal a cobra in a cage.

"Got him two days ago. Dumb kid had him as a pet!" Round of applause.

"Excellent. Sally?" Everyone turned to him, a small box on the table, red liquid seeping through the bottom.

"Head."

Thunder

#154

Soon as the first crack of thunder and flash of lightning illuminated the sky he remembered a similar day long ago.

He watched his wife sleep soundly and let his mind go back to their past twenty years together. They were the best years of his life.

He had no regrets about the deal he made that day twenty years ago. He should've died, instead he made a deal with death.

Twenty years to live his life as if they truly were his last. But nothing in this life is free. He would have no children.

Death was on time.

Cruel

#155

Hank glanced at himself in the rearview mirror for the fifth time. His hair was shinier than usual but the girl at the mall said it's what the ladies like to see.

Her house was larger than his, lush front yard, plus she still had both her parents to wait up for her on prom night.

He cut off his engine and grabbed a corsage from the passenger seat just as a limousine pulled up in front of him. She ran out, her prom dress shimmering by the light of the moon, grinned at Hank, then hopped in the limo.

Lost

#156

Little Timmy begged his mom for weeks to go to Toy Land. A store made just for children. All his friends from school had already been.

One day, she relented, even though she knew there would be nothing there she could afford to buy if he asked. Once inside the massive toy store, Timmy ran off to find the animatronic dinosaurs he'd seen in commercials.

Timmy never heard the loud speaker announcing the store was closing. Or the announcements earlier calling him to the nearest information booth.

They searched the store for days but little Timmy was never seen again.

Fall

#157

"What did I tell you about spying on the new neighbors?" Randall said, sneaking up on his wife, peeking through a gap in the privacy fence. "Where's my breakfast?"

Helen sucked her teeth and rolled her eyes at him. "Did you notice how late they were up last night?"

"No dear. I was asleep."

"I'm telling you, they were digging over there—"

"Gardening."

"In the middle of October?" She wanted to say more but stopped cold.

"Hope I didn't scare you," their neighbor said, perched on a step ladder, looking less alive than most. "We've been dying to get acquainted."

Hunger

#158

The way her body swayed to the rhythm of the music. Her hips hit every down beat and his missing heart skipped, breathless breath stopped. There was no one else in the room but her.

She wore a tight red dress, the color matching his hunger. He caught a glimpse of her neck beneath the flashing lights. He hadn't had a decent meal, a real meaty, pulsating, meal in three days.

His hands began to shake from nerves. She knew he craved her and taunted his desire from across the room. A stake hidden in the garter under her dress.

Poison

#159

"I'll bet you think you've got me, don't you?" Jimmy Lee said, sipping a cup of cocoa. Sitting across from him was Sheriff Hill who spent the better half of a decade hunting Jimmy. Outside were dozens of police cars and officers, their guns drawn. Exactly what he wanted.

"I know I do, Jimmy. This is the end of the road, so make this easier on all of us. Unburden your soul."

Jimmy took one more sip and said, "Funny thing about cocoa. It doesn't mask poison as well as you might think." He coughed once then lost his soul.

Dragon

#160

"Lose a dare, did ya?" Mrs. Walder asked, looking down at the little girl on her doorstep.

"No, miss," the young Girl Scout said. She was selling cookies door-to-door and Mrs. Walder was on her route.

"I know what you little heathens call me. Never to my face, of course. Well, what's the cookie no one ever buys? I'll take ten."

The girl's eyes widened and jaw dropped. She quickly offloaded ten boxes from her red wagon, took payment, and started to walk away.

She stopped, turned around, and shouted, "I don't think you're a dragon lady!" Then ran home.

Mask

#161

The line to get into the gallery wrapped around the building. Ever since we heard the painting was visiting, we all needed to get a glimpse of her.

Believed to be the first painting ever painted, it now traveled the world, giving everyone a chance to see her once before it was agreed by its owner and fellow investors that she needed to be locked away for preservation.

One week passed before it was my turn. I stared at her half-masked face. Her eyes just as captivating as I'd heard about from others.

Then she smiled and spoke my name.

Burn

#162

As the embers burned brightly under a full moon in the middle of a once quiet cul-de-sac, neighbors came out of their houses one-by-one, throwing something in as tribute to make the fire higher and hotter.

There was madness in their eyes as they threw in items once coveted and cherished. Now, just fuel for the flames.

In one home, a family stood at their window, shrouded in darkness, and watched. To the outside world they were not home to join in the merriment. Their eyes wept for the loss. A small child held her favorite book that much tighter.

Scalpel

#163

The lake was still. Not so much as a ripple in the water as the boat floated freely. Two passengers tried desperately not to stir. The early morning cold settled into their bones. Stiff as a board.

One pair of eyes fluttered closed. His friend grunted to keep his eyes open. It wouldn't work if one of them fell asleep. They both needed to bear witness.

The boat knocked to one side but they didn't move. Couldn't move?

It emerged from the water so quickly their boat capsized. Their eyes frozen open they watched its beauty, sinking towards the bottom.

Ghost

#164

My roommate is a ghost. Not what you expected me to say, I know. But that's the truth. When I agreed to buy it I was desperate. I should've known something wasn't right when the house was available dirt cheap. You gotta believe me.

The detective stopped the tape and stared at me. Arms folded. He leaned back in his chair. One spotlight hung low, barely illuminated the table.

"This is some story you've spun for my officers at the scene, Ms. Novak. Now, would you mind telling us who the dead man is that we found in your basement?"

Farm

#165

The Harrington Farm grand opening was in a few short hours and its owner prepared to let in the press early.

She checked her hair in a compact mirror and put it in her jacket pocket. She could see the media from her office window. The herd gathering. Quick footsteps down the hall stopped at her door and knocked softly.

"Enter," she said. Her assistant opened the door, out of breath, disheveled, dirt smeared on his face and clothes.

"We're ready."

"Excellent. Let them in." She put on a pair of metal fangs. "I think I'll join my babies tonight."

Caught

#166

"Well, this is unexpected, isn't it?" he said, waving a kitchen knife as he spoke. His wife and best friend, tied and gagged, looked on in terror. "When our neighbor, nosey Mr. Gallagher, asked if he could help my ailing wife, I asked what he meant. He knew who you were. What was going on. Threw it in my face."

He used the knife to pick up an apple and started cutting it into segments.

"See, he watched each and every time you showed up. 'Minutes after I had left,'" he said, making air quotes. "Clearly, this can't go on..."

Hostage

#167

Bobby clutched a photograph as the bank teller tapped away on her computer, glancing at him once. Twice. Then her eyes widened.

"Uhm, you're asking to withdraw twenty-thousand dollars today, sir?" Bobby nodded, choking back tears. He needed to be strong. He looked down at his best friend. A note pinned to him demanding money for his life. A fool's ransom. "I'll need to get my manager's approval for this amount."

Moments later the manager came out. "Please, I need the money to save his life." Bobby pressed the photograph against the glass partition, his caged pet pig, and bawled.

Children

#168

Ten year old Mandy banged her gavel slowly from behind a table used as the bench for a judge. Gathered around the backyard where the proceedings were taking place were all of the children from the town. Their parents watched from behind the fence line in silence.

"Will the accused please rise." Seated on a pair of tree stumps were Sally's parent's. They got to their feet, hoping to be found innocent. "For the crime of murder and hiding it with a goldfish imposter, the jury finds you..." Mandy turned to the jury of children, arms extended, thumbs down. "Guilty."

Risk

#169

"You know what you need in order to enter, Tom." The bookie didn't even look up. He already owed the boss a lot of money and his last ditch attempt at repayment would cost him more than the bookie thought he was willing to lose.

Tom pulled a photo from his wallet and thrust a shaky hand under the nose of the bookie who looked up with a smile. "Which one?"

With a quiver in his voice, Tom whispered, "the boy."

The bookie put a stamp over the boys face and handed back the photo. "I wish you luck, Tom."

Teeth

#170

For over a hundred years, on Halloween, children are warned to stay away from the Bower House. For twice as long it's been the home of Pete Bower. He may be over two hundred years old but on Halloween he feels like a kid again.

Pete's day begins at sunset. He rolls his aging body out of bed and shuffles to the bathroom. In the mirror he sees a youthful Pete and flashes a smile full of gums. From a metal tray on the sink he pops in a set of sharp, all steel dentures. Perfect for biting. CHOMP CHOMP!

Hide

#171

"Ready or not, here I come!" Gabe opened his eyes and took a step back from the tree he leaned against, letting his eyes adjust to the fog that arrived while he counted to ten.

He was scared and wanted to end the game but the last time he chickened out they teased him incessantly. He only had to find four of them. He took a deep breath and started the search in his backyard.

Inside the house Gabe's parent's watched him from their kitchen window. "Why can't he remember they're dead?"

"His therapist said it will take some time."

Ominous

#172

He smelled the smoke first. Then he ran to the window that had a direct view of the ominous house across the street.

"Someone's done it, honey!" His wife was already sitting on the couch in the living room, watching it became engulfed in flames. "Finally..."

She lit a cigarette to steady her shaky hand and calm her racing heartbeat. He turned to ask why she'd been so quiet but couldn't seem to find the words. An empty gasoline can at her feet.

"I wonder who the new neighbors might be now that the haunted house is gone?" she asked.

Chef

#173

"I'll give you a few minutes to look over the menu. If you have any questions—" The server started.

"We'd like to look at the after-hours menu," he said, handing back their menus to the waitress.

"Of course. We create the menu fresh each day. I'll be right back with that for you."

She returned with one menu that she placed on the table for them to read. It listed some notable and lesser known chefs.

"Look, honey, they have him today," his wife said, excitement in her voice.

"We'll have two large portions of chef Bouvier. Very well done."

Eerie

#174

As she walked into the antique shop, a bell rang over the door and she felt a chill up her spine. It was dark inside, except for a Victorian lamp dimming on the counter beside a register she bet never worked.

She was searching for something to buy her aunt. Not her favorite but now her only living relative. They hadn't seen each other in over two decades but she remembered her aunts love of creepy things.

Suddenly, she noticed an unusually large number of owl figurines everywhere and couldn't help but feel like they were watching her every move.

Shadow

#175

"Name?" I took a pair of latex gloves from the detective and knelt beside the body.

"Her name was Heather Motley. Forty-six. Married. Two children—"

"Damn it!" I said, getting to my feet. "How long have you been on the scene, detective Jones?"

"Uhm, t-t-two hours. Is there something wrong?"

I removed my glasses and pinched the top of my nose to try and calm myself before answering. "Yes, detective, there is something very wrong. Did I or did I not say I was to be called immediately whenever there is a dead body on the scene missing its shadow?"

Hounds

#176

She won't stop following me around. I'll admit I enjoyed the attention at first. Good looking stranger flirting with me at a party I never wanted to attend is a win in my book. That is, until she keeps showing up everywhere I go.

I'm trying to find the host so I can ask them who she is but there's too many people here. I need the bathroom.

I make a b-line upstairs and when I come out, there she is, waiting for me. I pretend to recognize someone behind her and walk right through her...

Wait...what just happened?

Doll

#177

One Sunday morning, Alice answered a knock at her front door and found a large rectangular box. No return address, just a note pinned on the box.

TAKE CARE.

She set aside the lid. Inside was a 3' porcelain doll with long auburn ringlets, wearing a pink dress. So pretty, Alice thought, assuming it must be a late birthday present from her sister. She placed it on a side table in her living room and never thought of it again.

"I'm hungry." The child's voice startled Alice awake. A girl in a pink dress at the foot of her bed.

Castle

#178

Usually, castles are found in fairytales, with damsels in distress high up in a tower, waiting for their prince to come and rescue them from the evil witch. This is not that tale.

On my way home I got caught in a storm, then a castle I had never seen before appeared out of a nowhere fog. Of course, it had no doors, what self-respecting castle would?

I found a vine and climbed in through an open window. If you hadn't guessed by now, I have been stuck in this damn tower for years.

Stop reading and send for help!

Scream

#179

"Interesting name for a diner, 'I Scream.' Does it have some deeper meaning?"

John barely glanced in her direction as he mindlessly wiped the counter in front of her. "If you're just passing through, I suggest you order something to go. It's not safe for a stranger to be here after dark."

"I guess that's why I'm the only one here. What do you recommend? I've been driving all day. I'm starving. I could eat my own arm right now."

John smiled. He pushed a button under counter. Doors locked. Large meat cleaver out. "That can be arranged."

She screamed!

Tattoo

#180

The letters first appeared on the inside of her left forearm. Some joke, she thought. A forgotten moment from last night's partying. She'd wash away the 'ur' and move on with her day.

With every scrub a new letter revealed, burned into her skin. A space then 'er.'

Then cuts appeared. She shoved her arm under the faucet to wash away the blood. Two more letters. With a shaky hand she dialed her best friend.

"We didn't go out last night, Dee."

The doorbell made her grab a kitchen knife. Another sharp pain. 'Murderer.' Doorbell rings again.

"Coming," she sings.

Full Moon

#181

Everyday, for the last forty-two days, I've come to The Full Moon Café at a quarter past two o'clock. I order the same drink. I sit at the same table. I pretend to read the same book. You might think I'm crazy. I'm sure the baristas here all talk about me. I hear their whispers.

I swear I xsaw a ghost that day. At least, it had to be a ghost because she's been dead now for twenty years. But there she was, sitting at a table, sipping a latte, staring like she recognized me. The man who killed her.

Levitation

#182

The Fowler's gathered round the newest member of their family, asleep in a bassinet, unaware of what was about to happen. The room grew silent when the matriarch entered, dressed in black from head to toe. Her potions bag draped over one shoulder.

She looked down at the child, her face concealed. She reached into her bag and pulled out a vial. She held it out over the child while everyone held hands, a deafening silence as she let one drop fall from the vial onto the sleeping child's head.

They were all smiles when the baby began to float.

Nightmare

#183

We built the nightmare room for one, shortly after we were approached with the opportunity of a lifetime. It would cost us nothing, at first. We didn't realize the cost needed mentally, to live with a demon in our minds three months at a time.

I didn't want it to be me again. I couldn't let it be her. She squeezed my hand then faced the panel, and gave a firm nod. She would suffer this time so I could find peace for a while.

They said we'd enjoy it after a while. We'll let you know when that happens.

Haunted House

#184

"I wish we had a haunted house on our street. Instead, we have this abandoned lot. No fun on Halloween."

"Be careful what you wish for, dude!" Best friends shove each other down the street past the empty lot.

"Dude! Wake up! Look out your damn window! Dude! I told your—"

"What is it?" he asked back over the walkie-talkie they used to chat with each other late into the night. He rubbed his eyes and walked over to his bedroom window.

"No way! No freaking way!"

In their jammies they raced to the lot where a house now stood.

Lady Tabitha

#185

"Do you often interrupt will readings with accusations of murder?" Lady Tabitha asked, surrounded by her four children.

"You will have to excuse me, Lady Tabitha, but I assume you want me to bring the killer of your husband to justice?"

She held out a cigarette for her doting son-in-law to light. "My dear inspector, whatever gave you that impression? Whoever killed him did us a favor. Are you suggesting one of us did it?"

"I don't make suggestions or accusations. I am absolutely sure of it. And you're next."

"I welcome death. I doubt the killer feels the same."

Sisters

#186

"Is she gone? Are you sure? Have you checked?" She held her sister's hand and squeezed it as she had every night for the past three nights that she visited.

"Yes, mum. She is no longer with us," the maid said, keeping a safe distance away.

Adrienne wasn't easily fooled. In one motion, she stuck a nearby threading needle into her sister's hand. No movement. A tremendous weight lifted. The only other person who knows is gone.

"Mum," said the maid, "she did have quite a lot to say before she left." Adrienne shook her head and laughed.

"B*tch."

Crazy

#187

I found this…thing…a few days ago. Hear me out because it might sound crazy. I still can't believe it myself. That crazy storm we had the other night. The one that knocked out power for miles around. Well, I was outside. Yes, I know, pouring rain. Crazy, right?

The sky…parted? Yeah, parted. And then there was this light. Not lightning. Just light. It was crazy. Cause next thing I know in my hand, this very hand, appeared this freaking paw. Like, why, I ask myself. Why me?

Ever since I got this my life has been…

Crazy!

Roids

#188

"How long will he be asleep?"

"Just two years, two months and two days," the nurse said, emotionless. They were all that way here. I hate 'Roids, but it was my father's request. He didn't want to die.

They promise an eternal life. More like an eternal death. What will he do once I'm gone? I squeeze his hand one last time before he wakes up one of them.

They say he won't even notice the changes. 20% is all they have been allowed to do to us. Give it time. We'll all be 100%. Forgetting how we got here.

Isolation

#189

They locked me in this room immediately after the verdict. I was found innocent but they weren't about to take any chances. Not with me. Not now.

I've been locked in this room, shrouded in darkness, no windows, for so long I've forgotten what day and night and time is.

I don't even remember what I did to be put in this damn room. I'm tired. I'm hungry. I haven't seen another human…

I'll go mad. I know it. Are my eyes open or closed? I lost my voice from the screaming. Why am I here? Who am I, again?

Hunger

#190

She noticed the change while eating lunch in the park one afternoon. A chicken parm sandwich. It was her favorite. But she didn't want it. In fact, the smell activated her gag reflexes in ways she never experienced before.

While throwing away her lunch she noticed a passerby's neck and her stomach grumbled at the sight. She licked her lips. Her salivary glands activated.

Before she could stop herself she started staring at everyone who walked by her differently. Like they were a meal instead of people.

That vampire she hooked up with last night told her this would happen.

Soil

#191

The trouble with telling a lie is remembering it the same way every time.

"When was the last time you spoke with Terry?" A rather nice police officer making the rounds after my neighbor has been missing for three days.

"A week ago, maybe? She was in her front yard working on her flowerbeds, I think…"

Not true. I couldn't possibly have seen her last week. At least not in her front yard. It was last week that I invited her for coffee. Nosey woman couldn't resist a chance to see inside my house.

She's inspecting my garden soil now.

Wallpaper

#192

There's nothing in the room except this ghastly wallpaper. No window to stare out of mindlessly. No books to get lost in. Just the sound of my own heart beating inside my head.

I'm supposed to be relaxing. Relieving my mind of the stress and burdens I put upon myself "out there." Whatever that means. Instead, I'm fixated on this wallpaper. Tears that were not there a moment ago are suddenly everywhere.

Someone is trying to escape. Is someone else in here with me? I close my eyes. Open them. My fingernails are bloodied from the scratching.

LET ME OUT!

The Election

#193

TODAY IS A GREAT DAY FOR ALL OF US. CONNOR SANTIAGO HAS WON THE ELECTION.

Loudspeakers on public transportation and on every high-rise building blared this message over and over again to anyone and everyone who cared to listen. Grown men in the streets cried with overwhelming joy. Women visited houses of worship to thank their Lord for such good news.

Just one household did not have the same reaction as the world, and that was the Santiagos. Connor sat at home, surrounded by friends and family.

His mother cried and squeezed his hand till the knock at the door.

The Sea

#194

The choppy seas rocked the boat so vigorously men were thrown overboard, and the lower deck was never dry.

At night Lessida paced the ship while grown men snored beneath her. The threat of nightmares wouldn't let her rest.

A wet hand grabbed her by the wrist and spun her in place. "You shouldn't be up here, miss. Not in your condition."

He glanced at her nightgown, open from the wind whipping about them. A scar where her heart should be, held closed by a row of haphazard stitches.

She closed her gown in embarrassment. Tears mixing with the sea.

Flat Tire

#195

I disarm them first, feed them some line about being a woman and how I've never changed a tire before. Gets them every time. Gives them a sense of being useful. Indeed.

I take this time to size them up. While they're down on their knees, doing whatever men do to fix a flat tire. Easy enough to do if you know how. Then I wait patiently on the side of the road and voila!

My mother keeps telling me it's no way to find a husband. Tell that to my last two. Third times a charm. Mark my words.

Blind

#196

I was born with no sight but I've always gotten around pretty good. My mother said I would outlive them all and she was right.

Now I am alone, forced to fend for myself. Until I got caught. It was my fault. I was greedy and hungry. A dangerous combination when you're my size but I gotta eat too!

The trap was set, knowing I would sniff out my favorite food; pizza. There's just something about the combination sauce, cheese and crust that gets me every time.

It was almost worth it die in the folds of a paper towel.

Mother

#197

The cave was dark and musty, as if time and air had stood still far from the world of human influence. It was a cave believed to contain the bones of a dragon. But not just any dragon, the mother of them all.

Not wanting her babies to live a life of service to man, she laid her body down on her last eggs, praying they would never hatched.

The expedition followed the map and entered the cave, expecting to find her bones. Instead, they encountered her flesh and bone, breathing. Sleeping.

She lived to protect them. Her eyes opened.

Man

#198

I must write my story. A testament to the great things I have done. My children will look back at my words and be amazed that their father has done so much! Oh, that they should accomplish as much as I have.

I've… I've…

Well, the list is so long I hardly know where to begin! Probably the beginning? My first accomplishment. The moment I knew I'd done something to be proud of.

"Still wasting time thinking about what you're going to write instead of just writing."

"I'm waiting for brilliance to come."

"That'll be a long wait," she said.

Home

#199

"Where are we?" he asked, peering through a thick fog, trying to see something in the distance. "Did it work?"

She had not spoken a word since they landed. It was his invention but her idea to go back. She needed to at least try and change what happened. For both of their sakes.

"Yes," she whispered to herself as the lights of the harbor came into view. She could hear the familiar bell of a ship coming in. The smell of the sea filled her with joy. "We did it, Jacob. We're home. And this time we'll find it."

Radio

#200

The words coming through the radio were garbled as he turned the dial slowly, trying to get a clearer signal again.

"Hello. Are you there?" he spoke into the microphone.

Static and indecipherable language, but nothing he could make out. He thought he heard the words "help" and "killer" which terrified him. It was believed a serial killer found his victims this way.

There it was again. The far away voice. "Help— He's coming for you—"

"Wait, who's coming? Who are you?"

What sounded like static soon became distinct laughter. He unplugged the radio but the laughter just grew louder.

"Write a short story every week. It's not possible to write 52 bad stories in a row."

— Ray Bradbury

to be continued...

themes index

Themes are how I come up with the ideas for the stories you've just read. I hope knowing this information will help you better understand why I wrote each one and you'll go back to reread and see how they are uniquely connected.

Story #101 - #106

Suit of Ink (Literary Tarot) | Pages 10 - 21

Brink Literacy Project, is a nonprofit organization dedicated to changing the world through storytelling. The Literary Tarot, brings together some of the greatest authors and cartoonists of our time to pair a tarot card with a seminal book that embodies the meaning of the arcana.

Nine of Ink - "The Most Dangerous Game" by Richard Connell - pg. 10
Ten of Ink - The Scarlet Letter: A Romance by Nathaniel Hawthorne - pg. 12
Page of Ink - The Magic Mountain by Thomas Mann - pg. 14
Knight of Ink - The Adventures of Huckleberry Fin by Mark Twain - pg. 16
Queen of Ink - Pride and Prejudice by Jane Austen - pg. 18
King of Ink - The War of the Worlds by H. G. Wells - pg. 20

Story #107 - #123

Newsletter Publication Names | Pages 22 - 55

Newsletters that inspired me to write a story based on their clever name. Without these amazing people who are all writing some truly great fiction, these stories would not exist. I encourage you to Google every one of them and subscribe to their newsletter to get even more amazing stories delivered to your inbox.

(Note: Some of these newsletters may no longer exist by the time this book is published.)

Brink Literacy Project, is a nonprofit organization dedicated to changing the world through storytelling. The Literary Tarot, brings together some of the greatest authors and cartoonists of our time to pair a tarot card with a seminal book that embodies the meaning of the arcana.

Newsletters that inspired me to write a story based on their clever name. Without these amazing people who are all writing some truly great fiction, these stories would not exist. I encourage you to Google every one of them and subscribe to their newsletter to get even more amazing stories delivered to your inbox.

(Note: Some of these newsletters may no longer exist by the time this book is published.)

Story #147 - #184

Pentober | Pages 102 - 177

An annual event and challenge for the fiction writing community that I invented as a way to get writers to use a pen and paper to write a story instead of technology. A word prompt is provided for participants to interpret however they like for the challenge. This is its first year.

Suit of Quills (Literary Tarot) | Pages 178 - 205

Brink Literacy Project, is a nonprofit organization dedicated to changing the world through storytelling. The Literary Tarot, brings together some of the greatest authors and cartoonists of our time to pair a tarot card with a seminal book that embodies the meaning of the arcana.

Newsletters that inspired me to write a story based on their clever name. Without these amazing people who are all writing some truly great fiction, these stories would not exist. I encourage you to Google every one of them and subscribe to their newsletter to get even more amazing stories delivered to your inbox.

(Note: Some of these newsletters may no longer exist by the time this book is published.)

The Xen'in Universe by Alex S. Garcia, pg. 206
Gibberish by Scoot, pg. 208

The Third 100

You've just read one hundred stories. Unless you also purchased The First 100. In which case you've read two hundred stories. But why stop there? I definitely didn't stop there. And I guarantee you don't have to look very far to find The Third 100 book to add to your shelf.

In this book I get to mix some of my loves; Christmas and the Twilight Zone. Together they allow me to flex my creative muscles and write some truly wild stories. Santa Claus meets Rod Serling. What could be better than that? Oh, right, me writing 100 word stories.

acknowledgements

There have been so many people along the way who've encouraged me and given me confidence when I was beginning to doubt my ability to keep up with writing a story every day.

All of you are far too many to name but to the Substack fiction writing community; thank you. For indulging my habit and even joining me on many collaborative efforts. They truly made a difference to me on a daily basis.

I also want to give thanks to Kickstarter and the many projects I've funded throughout the years. They have served me well in times of need.

about me

Erica L. Drayton was born in the Bronx, in NYC. She began writing stories almost immediately after she learned how to read and write from her mother, a former English teacher. As a gay, black, woman, Erica used storytelling as a way to express her feelings through poetry and fantasy novels at a young age.

After college, she took her continued passion for storytelling and developed it further, into writing short stories, eventually challenging herself to write 100 word stories.

She lives with her wife, young son, two dogs, and eight chickens in the Capital Region of Upstate New York.

erica drayton writes

Erica Drayton Writes is a newsletter that sends daily 100 Word Stories as well as updates on her countless other writing projects. She doesn't just write 100 word stories every single day. If that weren't enough, she also does all she can to inspire others to write 100 word stories on a regular basis.

If you subscribe today, you will receive a story every day that will make you think and one day give you the bug to try your own storytelling.

You can also upgrade for access to her comprehensive archive of 100 word stories, serials, and much more.